CHEESE

BY

ETHEL LINA WHITE

British Library Cataloguing-in-Publication Data
A catalogue record for this book is available from the
British Library

CONTENTS

ETHEL LINA WHITE

Ethel Lina White was born in Born in Abergavenny, Wales in 1876. She started writing as a child, contributing essays and poems to children's papers. For many years, she worked at the Ministry of Pensions in London, but she quit in her late forties in order to pursue writing. Her first three works, published between 1927 and 1930, were mainstream novels. Her first crime novel, published in 1931, was *Put Out the Light*. From this point onwards, White was a prolific author, and became one of the best-known crime writers in Britain and the US during the thirties and forties. Her novels *Some Must Watch* and *The Wheel Spins* were both made into popular films, as *The Spiral Staircase* and *The Lady Vanishes* respectively. Her 1942 novel *Midnight House* was adapted into *The Unseen* (1945), based on a screenplay co-authored by Raymond Chandler. White died in London in 1944, aged 68.

CHEESE

ETHEL LINA WHITE

This story begins with a murder. It ends with a mousetrap.

The murder can be disposed of in a paragraph. An attractive girl, carefully reared and educated for a future which held only a twisted throat. At the end of seven months, an unsolved mystery and a reward of £500.

It is a long way from a murder to a mouse-trap – and one with no finger-posts; but the police knew every inch of the way. In spite of a prestige punctured by the press and public, they had solved the identity of the killer. There remained the problem of tracking this wary and treacherous rodent from his unknown sewer in the underworld into their trap.

They failed repeatedly for lack of the right bait.

And unexpectedly, one spring evening, the bait turned up in the person of a young girl.

Cheese.

Inspector Angus Duncan was alone in his office when

her message was brought up. He was a red-haired Scot, handsome in a dour fashion, with the chin of a prize-fighter and keen blue eyes.

He nodded.

'I'll see her.'

It was between the lights. River, government offices and factories were all deeply dyed with the blue stain of dusk. Even in the city, the lilac bushes showed green tips and an occasional crocus cropped through the grass of the public-gardens, like strewn orange-peel. The evening star was a jewel in the pale green sky.

Duncan was impervious to the romance of the hour. He knew that twilight was but the prelude to night and that darkness was a shield for crime.

He looked up sharply when his visitor was admitted. She was young and flower-faced – her faint freckles already fading away into pallor. Her black suit was shabby, but her hat was garnished for the spring with a cheap cowslip wreath.

As she raised her blue eyes, he saw that they still carried the memory of country sweets . . . Thereupon he looked at her more sharply for he knew that of all poses, innocence is easiest to counterfeit.

'You say Roper sent you?' he enquired.

'Yes, Maggie Roper.'

He nodded. Maggie Roper – Sergeant Roper's niece – was

already shaping as a promising young Stores' detective.

'Where did you meet her?'

'At the Girls' Hostel where I'm staying.'

'Your name?'

'Jenny Morgan.'

'From the country?'

'Yes. But I'm up now for good.'

For good? . . . He wondered.

'Alone?'

'Yes.'

'How's that?' He looked at her mourning. 'People all dead?'

She nodded. From the lightning sweep of her lashes, he knew that she had put in some rough work with a tear. It prejudiced him in her favour. His voice grew more genial as his lips relaxed.

'Well, what's it all about?'

She drew a letter from her bag.

'I'm looking for work and I advertised in the paper. I got this answer. I'm to be companion-secretary to a lady, to travel with her and be treated as her daughter – if she likes me. I sent my photograph and my references and she's fixed an appointment.'

'When and where?'

'The day after tomorrow, in the First Room in the National

Gallery. But as she's elderly, she is sending her nephew to drive me to her house.'

'Where's that?'

She looked troubled.

'That's what Maggie Roper is making the fuss about. First, she said I must see if Mrs Harper – that's the lady's name – had taken up my references. And then she insisted on ringing up the Ritz where the letter was written from. The address was *printed*, so it was bound to be genuine, wasn't it?'

'Was it? What happened then?'

'They said no Mrs Harper had stayed there. But I'm sure it must be a mistake.' Her voice trembled. 'One must risk something to get such a good job.'

His face darkened. He was beginning to accept Jenny as the genuine article.

'Tell me,' he asked, 'have you had any experience of life?'

'Well, I've always lived in the country with Auntie. But I've read all sorts of novels and the newspapers.'

'Murders?'

'Oh, I love those.'

He could tell by the note in her childish voice that she ate up the newspaper accounts merely as exciting fiction, without the slightest realisation that the printed page was grim fact. He could see the picture: a sheltered childhood passed amid green spongy meadows. She could hardly cull sophistication from clover and cows.

'Did you read about the Bell murder?' he asked abruptly.

'Auntie wouldn't let me.' She added in the same breath, 'Every word.'

'Why did your aunt forbid you?'

'She said it must be a specially bad one, because they'd left all the bad parts out of the paper.'

'Well, didn't you notice the fact that that poor girl – Emmeline Bell – a well-bred girl of about your own age, was lured to her death through answering a newspaper advertisement?'

'I – I suppose so. But those things don't happen to oneself.'

'Why? What's there to prevent your falling into a similar trap?'

'I can't explain. But if there was something wrong, I should know it.'

'How? D'you expect a bell to ring or a red light to flash "Danger"?'

'Of course not. But if you believe in right and wrong, surely there must be some warning.'

He looked sceptical. That innocence bore a lily in its hand, was to him a beautiful phrase and nothing more. His own position in the sorry scheme of affairs was, to him, proof positive of the official failure of guardian angels.

'Let me see that letter, please,' he said.

She studied his face anxiously as he read, but his expression remained inscrutable. Twisting her fingers in her suspense, she glanced around the room, noting vaguely the three telephones on the desk and the stacked files in the pigeon-holes. A Great Dane snored before the red-caked fire. She wanted to cross the room and pat him, but lacked the courage to stir from her place.

The room was warm, for the windows were opened only a couple of inches at the top. In view of Duncan's weather-tanned colour, the fact struck her as odd.

Mercifully, the future is veiled. She had no inkling of the fateful part that Great Dane was to play in her own drama, nor was there anything to tell her that a closed window would have been a barrier between her and the yawning mouth of hell.

She started as Duncan spoke.

'I want to hold this letter for a bit. Will you call about this time tomorrow? Meantime, I must impress upon you the need of utmost caution. Don't take one step on your own. Should anything fresh crop up, 'phone me immediately. Here's my number.'

When she had gone, Duncan walked to the window. The blue dusk had deepened into a darkness pricked with lights. Across the river, advertisement-signs wrote themselves intermittently in coloured beads.

He still glowed with the thrill of the hunter on the first spoor of the quarry. Although he had to await the report of the expert test, he was confident that the letter which he held had been penned by the murderer of poor ill-starred Emmeline Bell.

Then his elation vanished at a recollection of Jenny's wistful face. In this city were scores of other girls, frail as windflowers too – blossom-sweet and country-raw – forced through economic pressure into positions fraught with deadly peril.

The darkness drew down overhead like a dark shadow pregnant with crime. And out from their holes and sewers stole the rats . . .

At last Duncan had the trap baited for his rat.

A young and pretty girl – ignorant and unprotected. Cheese.

When Jenny, punctual to the minute, entered his office, the following evening, he instantly appraised her as his prospective decoy. His first feeling was one of disappointment. Either she had shrunk in the night or her eyes had grown bigger. She looked such a frail scrap as she stared at him, her lips bitten to a thin line, that it seemed hopeless to credit her with the necessary nerve for his project.

'Oh, please tell me it's all perfectly right about

that letter.'

'Anything but right.'

For a moment, he thought she was about to faint. He wondered uneasily whether she had eaten that day. It was obvious from the keenness of her disappointment that she was at the end of her resources.

'Are you sure?' she insisted. 'It's – very important to me. Perhaps I'd better keep the appointment. If I didn't like the look of things, I needn't go on with it.'

'I tell you, it's not a genuine job,' he repeated. 'But I've something to put to you that is the goods. Would you like to have a shot at £500?'

Her flushed face, her eager eyes, her trembling lips, all answered him.

'Yes, please,' was all she said.

He searched for reassuring terms.

'It's like this. We've tested your letter and know it is written, from a bad motive, by an undesirable character.'

'You mean a criminal?' she asked quickly.

'Um. His record is not good. We want to get hold of him.'

'Then why don't you?'

He suppressed a smile.

'Because he doesn't confide in us. But if you have the courage to keep your appointment tomorrow and let his messenger take you to the house of the suppositious Mrs Harper, I'll guarantee it's the hiding-place of the man we want. We get him – you get the reward. Question is – have you the nerve?'

She was silent. Presently she spoke in a small voice.

'Will I be in great danger?'

'None. I wouldn't risk your safety for any consideration. From first to last, you'll be under the protection of the Force.'

'You mean I'll be watched over by detectives in disguise?'

'From the moment you enter the National Gallery, you'll be covered doubly and trebly. You'll be followed every step of the way and directly we've located the house, the place will be raided by the police.'

'All the same, for a minute or so, just before you can get into the house, I'll be alone with – *him*?'

'The briefest interval. You'll be safe at first. He'll begin with overtures. Stall him off with questions. Don't let him see you suspect – or show you're frightened.'

Duncan frowned as he spoke. It was his duty to society to rid it of a dangerous pest and in order to do so, Jenny's cooperation was vital. Yet, to his own surprise, he disliked the necessity in the case of this especial girl.

'Remember we'll be at hand,' he said. 'But if your nerve goes, just whistle and we'll break cover immediately.'

'Will *you* be there?' she asked suddenly.

'Not exactly in the foreground. But I'll be there.'

'Then I'll do it.' She smiled for the first time. 'You laughed at me when I said there was something inside me which told me – things. But I just know I can trust *you*.'

'Good.' His voice was rough. 'Wait a bit. You've been put to expense coming over here. This will cover your fares and so on.'

He thrust a note into her hand and hustled her out, protesting. It was a satisfaction to feel that she would eat that night. As he seated himself at his desk, preparatory to work, his frozen face was no index of the emotions raised by Jenny's parting words.

Hitherto, he had thought of women merely as 'skirts'. He had regarded a saucepan with an angry woman at the business end of it, merely as a weapon. For the first time he had a domestic vision of a country girl – creamy and fragrant as meadowsweet – in a nice womanly setting of saucepans.

Jenny experienced a thrill which was almost akin to exhilaration when she entered Victoria station, the following day. At the last moment, the place for meeting had been altered in a telegram from 'Mrs Harper'.

Immediately she had received the message, Jenny had gone to the telephone-box in the hostel and duly reported the change of plan, with a request that her message should be repeated to her, to obviate any risk of mistake.

And now – the incredible adventure was actually begun.

The station seemed filled with hurrying crowds as she walked slowly towards the clock. Her feet rather lagged on the way. She wondered if the sinister messenger had already marked the yellow wreath in her hat which she had named as her mark of identification.

Then she remembered her guards. At this moment they were here, unknown, watching over her slightest movement. It was a curious sensation to feel that she was spied upon by unseen eyes. Yet it helped to brace the muscles of her knees when she took up her station under the clock with the sensation of having exposed herself as a target for gunfire.

Nothing happened. No one spoke to her. She was encouraged to gaze around her . . .

A few yards away, a pleasant-faced smartly dressed young man was covertly regarding her. He carried a yellowish sample-bag which proclaimed him a drummer.

Suddenly Jenny felt positive that this was one of her guards. There was a quality about his keen clean-shaven face – a hint of the eagle in his eye – which reminded her of Duncan. She gave him the beginnings of a smile and was thrilled when, almost imperceptibly, he fluttered one eyelid. She read it as a signal for caution. Alarmed by her indiscretion, she looked fixedly in another direction.

Still – it helped her to know that even if she could not see him, he was there.

The minutes dragged slowly by. She began to grow anxious as to whether the affair were not some hoax. It would be not only a tame ending to the adventure but a positive disappointment. She would miss the chance of a sum which – to her – was a little fortune. Her need was so vital that she would have undertaken the venture for five pounds. Morever, after her years of green country solitude, she felt a thrill at the mere thought of her temporary link with the underworld. This was life in the raw; while screening her as she aided him, she worked with Angus Duncan.

She smiled – then started as though stung.

Someone had touched her on the arm.

'Have I the honour, happiness and felicity of addressing Miss Jenny Morgan? Yellow wreath in the lady's hat. Red Flower in the gent's buttonhole, as per arrangement.'

The man who addressed her was young and bull-necked, with florid colouring which ran into blotches. He wore a red carnation in the buttonhole of his check overcoat.

'Yes, I'm Jenny Morgan.'

As she spoke, she looked into his eyes. She felt a sharp revulsion – an instinctive recoil of her whole being.

'Are you Mrs Harper's nephew?' she faltered.

'That's right. Excuse a gent keeping a lady waiting, but I

just slipped into the bar for a glass of milk. I've a taxi waiting if you'll just hop outside.'

Jenny's mind worked rapidly as she followed him. She was forewarned and protected. But – were it not for Maggie Roper's intervention – she would have kept this appointment in very different circumstances. She wondered whether she would have heeded that instinctive warning and refused to follow the stranger.

She shook her head. Her need was so urgent that, in her wish to believe the best, she knew that she would have summoned up her courage and flouted her fears as nerves. She would have done exactly what she was doing – accompanying an unknown man to an unknown destination.

She shivered at the realisation. It might have been herself. Poor defenceless Jenny – going to her doom.

At that moment she encountered the grave scrutiny of a stout clergyman who was standing by the book-stall. He was ruddy, wore horn-rimmed spectacles and carried the *Church Times*.

His look of understanding was almost as eloquent as a vocal message. It filled her with gratitude. Again she was certain that this was a second guard. Turning to see if the young commercial traveller were following her, she was thrilled to discover that he had preceded her into the station yard. He got into a taxi at the exact moment that her companion flung open the door of a cab which was waiting. It was only this knowledge that Duncan was thus making good his promise which induced her to enter the vehicle. Once again her nerves rebelled and she was rent with sick forebodings.

As they moved off, she had an overpowering impulse to scream aloud for help to the porters – just because all this might have happened to some poor girl who had not her own good fortune.

Her companion nudged her.

'Bit of all right, joy-riding, eh?'

She stiffened, but managed to force a smile.

'Is it a long ride?'

'Ah, now you're asking.'

'Where does Mrs Harper live?'

'Ah, that's telling.'

She shrank away, seized with disgust of his blotched face so near her own.

'Please give me more room. It's stifling here.'

'Now, don't you go taking no liberties with me. A married man I am, with four wives all on the dole.' All the same, to her relief, he moved further away. 'From the country, aren't you? Nice place. Lots of milk. Suit me a treat. Any objection to a gent smoking?'

'I wish you would. The cab reeks of whisky.'

They were passing St Paul's which was the last landmark in her limited knowledge of London. Girls from offices passed on the pavement, laughing and chatting together, or hurrying by intent on business. A group was scattering crumbs to the pigeons which fluttered on the steps of the cathedral.

She watched them with a stab of envy. Safe happy girls.

Then she remembered that somewhere, in the press of traffic, a taxi was shadowing her own. She took fresh courage.

The drive passed like an interminable nightmare in which she was always on guard to stem the advances of her disagreeable companion. Something seemed always on the point of happening – something unpleasant, just out of sight and round the corner – and then, somehow she staved it off.

The taxi bore her through a congested maze of streets. Shops and offices were succeeded by regions of warehouses and factories, which in turn gave way to areas of dun squalor where gas-works rubbed shoulders with grimed laundries which bore such alluring signs as DEWDROP or WHITE ROSE.

From the shrilling of sirens, Jenny judged that they were in the neighbourhood of the river, when they turned into a quiet square. The tall lean houses wore an air of drab respectability. Lace curtains hung at every window. Plaster pineapples crowned the pillared porches.

'Here's our "destitution".'

As her guide inserted his key in the door of No. 17, Jenny glanced eagerly down the street, in time to see a taxi turn the corner.

'Hop in, dearie.'

On the threshold Jenny shrank back.

Evil.

Never before had she felt its presence. But she knew. Like the fumes creeping upwards from the grating of a sewer, it poisoned the air.

Had she embarked on this enterprise in her former ignorance, she was certain that at this point, her instinct would have triumphed.

'I would never have passed through this door.'

She was wrong. Volition was swept off the board. Her arm was gripped and before she could struggle, she was pulled inside.

She heard the slam of the door.

'Never loiter on the doorstep, dearie. Gives the house a bad name. This way. Up the stairs. All the nearer to heaven.'

Her heart heavy with dread, Jenny followed him. She had entered on the crux of her adventure – the dangerous few minutes when she would be quite alone.

The place was horrible – with no visible reason for horror.

It was no filthy East-end rookery, but a technically clean apartment-house. The stairs were covered with brown linoleum. The mottled yellow wallpaper was intact. Each landing had its marble-topped table, adorned with a forlorn aspidistra – its moulting rug at every door. The air was dead and smelt chiefly of dust.

They climbed four flights of stairs without meeting anyone. Only faint rustlings and whispers within the rooms told of other tenants. Then the blotched-faced man threw open a door.

'Young lady come to see Mrs Harper about the sitooation. Too-tel-oo, dearie. Hope you strike lucky.'

He pushed her inside and she heard his step upon the stairs.

In that moment, Jenny longed for anyone – even her late companion.

She was vaguely aware of the figure of a man seated in a chair. Too terrified to look at him, her eyes flickered around the room.

Like the rest of the house, it struck the note of parodied respectability. Yellowish lace curtains hung at the windows which were blocked by pots of leggy geraniums. A walnut-wood suite was upholstered in faded bottle-green rep with burst padding. A gilt-framed mirror surmounted a stained marble mantelpiece which was decorated with a clock –

permanently stopped under its glass case – and a bottle of whisky. On a small table by the door rested a filthy cage, containing a grey parrot, its eyes mere slits of wicked eld between wrinkled lids.

It had to come. With an effort, she looked at the man.

He was tall and slender and wrapped in a once-gorgeous dressing-gown of frayed crimson quilted silk. At first sight, his features were not only handsome but bore some air of breeding. But the whole face was blurred – as though it were a waxen mask half-melted by the sun and over which the Fiend – in passing – had lightly drawn a hand. His eyes drew her own. Large and brilliant, they were of so light a blue as to appear almost white. The lashes were unusually long and matted into spikes.

The blood froze at Jenny's heart. The girl was no fool. Despite Duncan's cautious statements, she had drawn her own deduction which linked an unsolved murder mystery and a reward of £500.

She knew that she was alone with a homicidal maniac – the murderer of ill-starred Emmeline Bell.

In that moment, she realised the full horror of a crime which, a few months ago, had been nothing but an exciting newspaper-story. It sickened her to reflect that a girl – much like herself – whose pretty face smiled fearlessly upon the world from the printed page, had walked into this same trap, in all the blindness of her youthful confidence. No one to hear her cries. No one to guess the agony of those last terrible moments.

Jenny at least understood that first rending shock of realisation. She fought for self-control. At sight of that smiling marred face, she wanted to do what she knew instinctively that other girl had done – precipitating her doom. With a desperate effort she suppressed the impulse to rush madly round the room like a snared creature, beating her hands against the locked door and crying for help. Help which would never come.

Luckily, common sense triumphed. In a few minutes' time, she would not be alone. Even then a taxi was speeding on its mission; wires were humming; behind her was the protection of the Force.

She remembered Duncan's advice to temporise. It was true that she was not dealing with a beast of the jungle which sprang on its prey at sight.

'Oh, please.' She hardly recognised the tiny pipe. 'I've come to see Mrs Harper about her situation.'

'Yes.' The man did not remove his eyes from her face. 'So you are Jenny?'

'Yes, Jenny Morgan. Is – is Mrs Harper in?'

'She'll be in presently. Sit down. Make yourself at home. What are you scared for?'

'I'm not scared.'

Her words were true. Her strained ears had detected faintest sounds outside – dulled footsteps, the cautious fastening of a door.

The man, for his part, also noticed the stir. For a few seconds he listened intently. Then to her relief, he relaxed his attention.

She snatched again at the fiction of her future employer.

'I hope Mrs Harper will soon come in.'

'What's your hurry? Come closer. I can't see you properly.'

They were face to face. It reminded her of the old nursery story of 'Little Red Riding Hood'.

'What big eyes you've got, Grandmother.'

The words swam into her brain.

Terrible eyes. Like white glass cracked in distorting facets. She was looking into the depths of a blasted soul. Down, down . . . That poor girl. But she must not think of *her*. She must be brave – give him back look for look.

Her lids fell . . . She could bear it no longer.

She gave an involuntary start at the sight of his hands. They were beyond the usual size – unhuman – with long knotted fingers.

'What big hands you've got.'

Before she could control her tongue, the words

slipped out.

The man stopped smiling.

But Jenny was not frightened now. Her guards were near. She thought of the detective who carried the bag of samples. She thought of the stout clergyman. She thought of Duncan.

At that moment, the commercial traveller was in an upper room of a wholesale drapery house in the city, holding the fashionable blonde lady buyer with his magnetic blue eye, while he displayed his stock of crêpe-de-Chine underwear.

At that moment, the clergyman was seated in a third-class railway carriage, watching the hollows of the Downs fill with heliotrope shadows. He was not quite at ease. His thoughts persisted on dwelling on the frightened face of a little country girl as she drifted by in the wake of a human vulture.

'I did wrong. I should have risked speaking to her.'

But – at that moment – Duncan was thinking of her.

Jenny's message had been received over the telephone wire, repeated and duly written down by Mr Herbert Yates, shorthand-typist – who, during the absence of Duncan's own secretary, was filling the gap for one morning. At the sound of his chief's step in the corridor outside, he rammed on his hat, for he was already overdue for a lunch appointment with one of the numerous 'only girls in the world'.

At the door he met Duncan.

'May I go to lunch now, sir?'

Duncan nodded assent. He stopped for a minute in the passage while he gave Yates his instructions for the afternoon.

'Any message?' he enquired.

'One come this instant, sir. It's under the weight.'

Duncan entered the office. But in that brief interval, the disaster had occurred.

Yates could not be held to blame for what happened. It was true that he had taken advantage of Duncan's absence to open a window wide, but he was ignorant of any breach of rules. In his hurry he had also written down Jenny's message on the nearest loose-leaf to hand, but he had taken the precaution to place it under a heavy paper-weight.

It was Duncan's Great Dane which worked the mischief. He was accustomed at this hour to be regaled with a biscuit by Duncan's secretary who was an abject dog-lover. As his dole had not been forthcoming he went in search of it. His great paws on the table, he rooted among the papers, making nothing of a trifle of a letter-weight. Over it went. Out of the window – at the next gust – went Jenny's message. Back to his rug went the dog.

The instant Duncan was aware of what had happened, a frantic search was made for Yates. But that wily and athletic youth, wise to the whims of his official superiors, had disappeared. They raked every place of refreshment within a wide radius. It was not until Duncan's men rang up to report that they had drawn a blank at the National Gallery, that Yates was discovered in an underground dive, drinking coffee and smoking cigarettes with his charmer.

Duncan arrived at Victoria forty minutes after the appointed time.

It was the bitterest hour of his life. He was haunted by the sight of Jenny's flower-face upturned to his. She had *trusted* him. And in his ambition to track the man he had taken advantage of her necessity to use her as a pawn in his game.

He had played her – and lost her.

The thought drove him to madness. Steeled though he was to face reality, he dared not to let himself think of the end. Jenny – country-raw and blossom-sweet – even then struggling in the grip of murderous fingers.

Even then.

Jenny panted as she fought, her brain on fire. The thing had rushed upon her so swiftly that her chief feeling was of sheer incredulity. What had gone before was already burning itself up in a red mist. She had no clear memory afterwards of those tense minutes of fencing. There was only an interlude filled with a dimly comprehended menace – and then this.

And still Duncan had not intervened.

Her strength was failing. Hell cracked, revealing glimpses of unguessed horror.

With a supreme effort she wrenched herself free. It was but a momentary respite, but it sufficed for her signal – a broken tremulous whistle.

The response was immediate. Somewhere outside the door a gruff voice was heard in warning.

'Perlice.'

The killer stiffened, his ears pricked, every nerve astrain. His eyes flickered to the ceiling which was broken by the outline of a trap-door.

Then his glance fell upon the parrot.

His fingers on Jenny's throat, he paused. The bird rocked on its perch, its eyes slits of malicious eld.

Time stood still. The killer stared at the parrot. Which of the gang had given the warning? Whose voice? Not Glasseye. Not Mexican Joe. The sound had seemed to be within the room.

That parrot.

He laughed. His fingers tightened. Tightened to relax.

For a day and a half he had been in Mother Bargery's room. During that time the bird had been dumb. Did it talk?

The warning echoed in his brain. Every moment of delay was fraught with peril. At that moment his enemies were here, stealing upwards to catch him in their trap. The instinct of the human rodent, enemy of mankind – eternally hunted and harried – prevailed. With an oath, he flung Jenny aside and jumping on the table, wormed through the trap of the door.

Jenny was alone. She was too stunned to think. There was still a roaring in her ears, shooting lights before her eyes. In a vague way, she knew that some hitch had occurred in the plan. The police were here – yet they had let their prey escape.

She put on her hat, straightened her hair. Very slowly she walked down the stairs. There was no sign of Duncan or of his men.

As she reached the hall, a door opened and a white puffed face looked at her. Had she quickened her pace or shown the least sign of fear she would never have left that place alive. Her very nonchalance proved her salvation as she unbarred the door with the deliberation bred of custom.

The street was deserted, save for an empty taxi which she hailed.

'Where to, miss?' asked the driver.

Involuntarily she glanced back at the drab house, squeezed into its strait-waistcoat of grimed bricks. She had a momentary vision of a white blurred face flattened against the glass. At the sight, realisation swept over her in wave upon wave of sick terror.

There had been no guards. She had taken every step of that perilous journey – alone.

Her very terror sharpened her wits to action. If her eyesight had not deceived her, the killer had already discovered that the alarm was false. It was obvious that he would not run the risk of remaining in his present quarters. But it was possible that he might not anticipate a lightning swoop; there was nothing to connect a raw country girl with a preconcerted alliance with a Force.

'The nearest telephone-office,' she panted. 'Quick.'

A few minutes later, Duncan was electrified by Jenny's voice gasping down the wire.

'He's at 17 Jamaica Square, SE. No time to lose. He'll go out through the roof . . . Quick, quick.'

'Right. Jenny, where'll you be?'

'At your house. I mean, Scot – Quick.'

As the taxi bore Jenny swiftly away from the dun outskirts, a shrivelled hag pattered into the upper room of that drab house. Taking no notice of its raging occupant, she approached the parrot's cage.

'Talk for mother, dearie.'

She held out a bit of dirty sugar. As she whistled, the parrot opened its eyes.

'Perlice.'

It was more than two hours later when Duncan entered his private room at Scotland Yard.

His eyes sought Jenny.

A little wan, but otherwise none the worse for her adventure, she presided over a teapot which had been provided by the resourceful Yates. The Great Dane – unmindful of a little incident of a letter-weight – accepted her biscuits and caresses with deep sighs of protest.

Yates sprang up eagerly.

'Did the cop come off, chief?'

Duncan nodded twice – the second time towards the door, in dismissal.

Jenny looked at him in some alarm when they were alone together. There was little trace left of the machine-made martinet of the Yard. The lines in his face appeared freshly re-tooled and there were dark pouches under his eyes.

'Jenny,' he said slowly, 'I've – sweated – blood.'

'Oh, was he so very difficult to capture? Did he fight?'

'Who? That rat? He ran into our net just as he was about to bolt. He'll lose his footing all right. No.'

'Then why are you—'

'*You*.'

Jenny threw him a swift glance. She had just been half-murdered after a short course of semi-starvation, but she commanded the situation like a lion tamer.

'Sit down,' she said, 'and don't say one word until you've drunk this.'

He started to gulp obediently and then knocked over his cup.

'Jenny, you don't know the hell I've been through. You don't understand what you ran into. That man—'

'He was a murderer, of course. I knew that all along.'

'But you were in deadliest peril—'

'I wasn't frightened, so it didn't matter. I knew I could trust you.'

'Don't Jenny. Don't turn the knife. I failed you. There was a ghastly blunder.'

'But it *was* all right, for it ended beautifully. You see, something told me to trust you. I always know.'

During his career, Duncan had known cases of love at first sight. So, although he could not rule them out, he always argued along Jenny's lines.

Those things did not happen to him.

He realised now that it had happened to him – cautious Scot though he was.

'Jenny,' he said, 'it strikes me that I want someone to watch *me*.'

'I'm quite sure you do. Have I won the reward?'

His rapture was dashed.

'Yes.'

'I'm so glad. I'm rich.' She smiled happily. 'So this can't be pity for me.'

'Pity? Oh, Jenny—'

Click. The mouse-trap was set for the confirmed bachelor with the right bait.

A young and friendless girl – homely and blossom-sweet.

Cheese.